DATE DUE

796.332
KEL   Kelley, K. C.
           Chicago Bears

3.6   no lex

White Rock Elementary

FAVORITE FOOTBALL TEAMS

CHICAGO BEARS

BY K. C. KELLEY

Property of
WHITE ROCK SCHOOL

The Child's World

THE CHILD'S WORLD®
1980 Lookout Drive • Mankato, MN 56003-1705
800-599-READ • www.childsworld.com

ACKNOWLEDGMENTS
The Child's World®: Mary Berendes, Publishing Director
Shoreline Publishing Group, LLC: James Buckley, Jr.,
 Production Director
The Design Lab: Kathleen Petelinsek, Design;
 Gregory Lindholm, Page Production

PHOTOS
Cover: Focus on Football
Interior: AP/Wide World: 9, 10, 17, 18, 21, 22 box; Final Shot
 Photography: 22 main; Focus on Football: 5, 6, 13, 25, 27;
 Stockexpert: 14

Published in the United States of America.
LIBRARY OF CONGRESS
CATALOGING-IN-PUBLICATION DATA
Kelley, K. C.
  Chicago Bears / by K.C. Kelley.
    p. cm. — (Favorite football teams)
  Includes bibliographical references and index.
  ISBN 978-1-60253-313-4 (library bound : alk. paper)
  1. Chicago Bears (Football team)—History—Juvenile literature.
I. Title. II. Series.
  GV956.C5K45 2009
  796.332'v640977311—dc22   2009009063

COPYRIGHT
Copyright © 2010 by The Child's World®.
All rights reserved. No part of this book may be
reproduced or utilized in any form or by any means
without written permission from the publisher.

TABLE OF CONTENTS

- **4** Go, Bears!
- **7** Who Are the Chicago Bears?
- **8** Where They Came From
- **11** Who They Play
- **12** Where They Play
- **15** The Football Field
- **16** Big Days!
- **19** Tough Days!
- **20** Meet the Fans
- **23** Heroes Then . . .
- **24** Heroes Now . . .
- **26** Gearing Up
- **28** Sports Stats
- **30** Glossary
- **31** Find Out More
- **32** Index/Author

FAVORITE FOOTBALL TEAMS

Go, Bears!

Real bears roar. Chicago Bears play football! Football fans in Chicago cheer for their favorite team. They watch the Bears at the stadium and on TV. The Bears have a long history in Chicago. Many great football heroes have played for the Bears. Are they your favorite team? Let's meet the Chicago Bears!

Here come the Bears! Chicago is always good on **defense**. Here's Mike Brown (30) returning an **interception** with help from his teammates.

5

6

CHICAGO BEARS

Who Are the Chicago Bears?

The Chicago Bears play in the National Football League (NFL). They are one of 32 teams in the NFL. The NFL includes the National Football Conference (NFC) and the American Football Conference (AFC). The Bears play in the North Division of the NFC. The winner of the NFC plays the winner of the AFC in the **Super Bowl**. The Bears have been the NFL champions nine times!

On this play, the Bears are lined up to try for a **field goal**. The player with the ball will snap, or throw it underhand, to the holder. The other guys will block!

FAVORITE FOOTBALL TEAMS

Where They Came From

The Bears were not always the Bears. In 1920, A. E. Staley started a pro football team. He called them the Decatur Staleys. Decatur is a city near Chicago. The Staley was a type of car. In 1921, George Halas bought the team. He moved it to nearby Chicago. The next year, he gave the team a new name—the Bears! Halas was also the coach of the team most of the time until 1968. No wonder they called him "Papa Bear!"

Here are three Chicago Bears stars from the late 1940s: Johnny Lujack, Sid Luckman, and Bobby Layne. Notice how their leather helmets did not have facemasks!

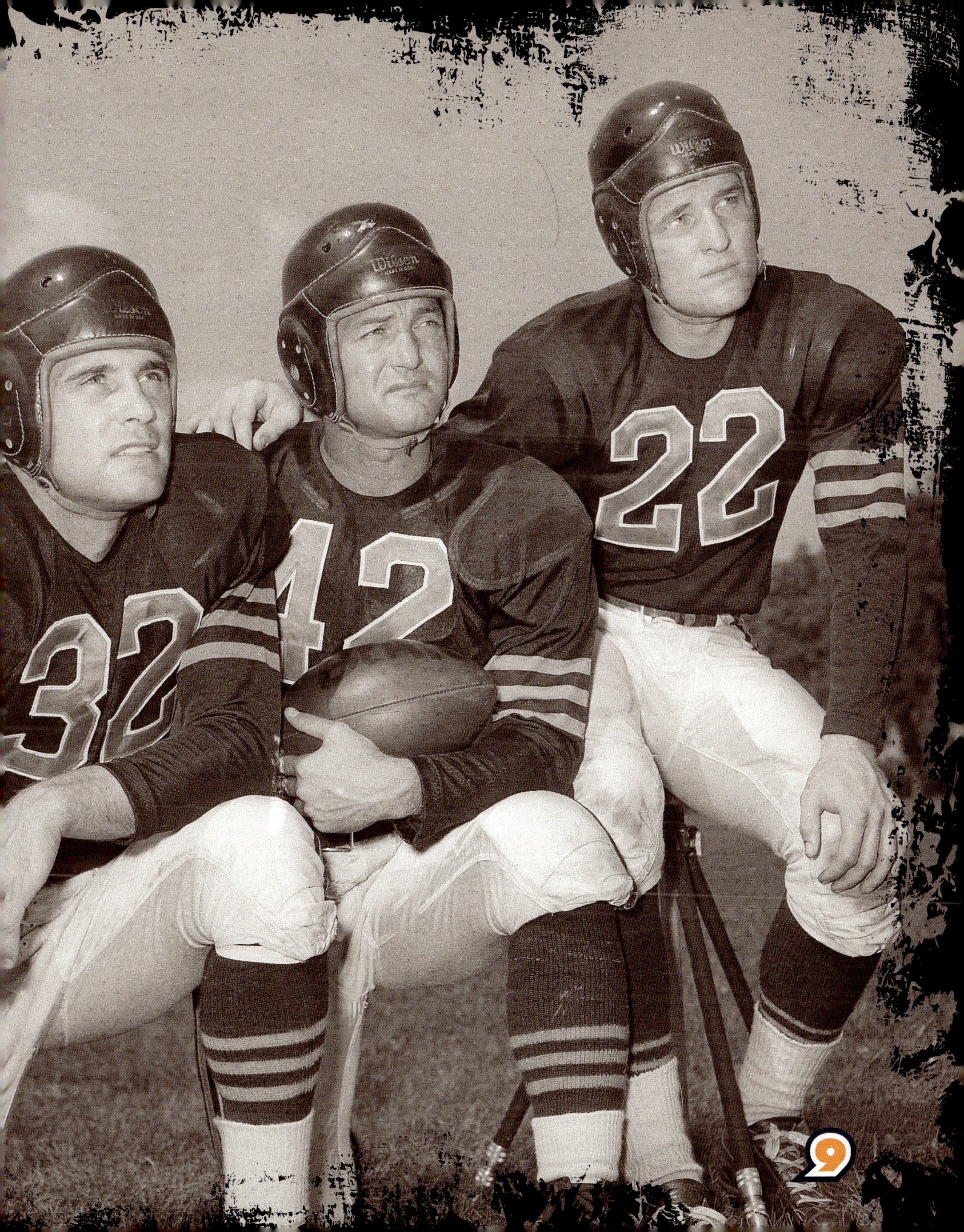
Wilson
Wilson
Wilson
32
42
22

10

CHICAGO BEARS

Who They Play

The Bears play 16 games each season. There are three other teams in the NFC North. They are the Green Bay Packers, the Minnesota Vikings, and the Detroit Lions. Every year, the Bears play each of these teams twice. They also play other teams in the NFC and AFC. The Bears and the Packers have been **rivals** since 1923. Their hard-hitting games are always fan favorites!

Games between the Bears and the Packers are always big battles. Here, Chicago's Brian Urlacher is bringing down a Green Bay runner in a 2008 game.

FAVORITE FOOTBALL TEAMS

Where They Play

The Bears play their home games at Soldier Field. This huge stadium is in downtown Chicago, on the Lake Michigan shore. Soldier Field opened in 1924. It is named for the men and women who served in the military during World War I. Huge stone pillars line one side of the stadium walls. The Bears did not start playing at Soldier Field until 1971. Before that, they played at Wrigley Field. Wrigley Field is famous as the home of baseball's Chicago Cubs.

In a strong wind off Lake Michigan, American flags flap above Soldier Field. Fans who watch games here often prepare to deal with cold weather.

SOLDIER FIELD
DEDICATED TO THE MEN AND WOMEN
OF THE ARMED SERVICES

FOOTBALL

- goalpost
- end zone
- red zone
- sideline
- midfield
- hash mark
- red zone
- goalpost
- end zone

CHICAGO BEARS

The Football Field

An NFL field is 100 yards long. At each end is an **end zone** that is another 10 yards deep. Short white **hash marks** on the field mark off every yard. Longer lines mark every five yards. Numbers on the field help fans know where the players are. Goalposts stand at the back of each end zone. On some plays, a team can kick the football through the goalposts to earn points. During the game, each team stands along one sideline of the field. Soldier Field is covered with real grass. Some indoor NFL stadiums use **artificial**, or fake, grass.

During a game, the two teams stand on the sidelines. They usually stand near midfield, waiting for their turns to play. Coaches walk on the sidelines, too, along with cheerleaders and photographers.

FAVORITE FOOTBALL TEAMS

Big Days!

The Chicago Bears have had many great moments in their long history. Here are three of the greatest:

1940: The Bears beat the Washington Redskins 73–0 to win the NFL title. That's still a record for the most points scored in one game!

1963: George Halas won the last of his eight NFL championships as a coach. The Bears beat the New York Giants 14–10.

1986: The Bears won Super Bowl XX. They beat the New England Patriots 46–10. This mighty Bears team was one of the greatest of all time. Chicago won every game that season except one.

We won! Here, coach Mike Ditka is carried off the field after the Bears win in Super Bowl XX. It's a great way to leave a football field!

17

18

CHICAGO BEARS

Tough Days!

The Bears can't win all their games. Some games or seasons don't turn out well. The players keep trying to play their best, though! Here are some painful memories from Bears history:

1968: Star **running back** Gale Sayers hurt his knee very badly. He played several more seasons, but he was never as fast or as good as he had been.

1969: The Bears won only one game—it was their worst season ever!

1983: George Halas died at the age of 88. He was part of the Bears longer than anyone had ever been part of one team.

Oops! Gale Sayers lost the ball on this play. However, he was one of the greatest players in Bears history.

FAVORITE FOOTBALL TEAMS

Meet the Fans

Fans all over the Chicago area root for the Bears. They often use a nickname for their favorite team: "Da Bears!" Bears fans must be very tough. In the winter, games at Soldier Field can be very cold. Fans and players alike must bundle up to protect themselves. Along with cold, they might deal with fog. In a 1988 game, the fog got so thick that fans in the higher seats couldn't see the field!

Staying warm at Bears games is important. But so is wearing Bears gear! This fan makes sure to cover up with lots of blue and orange!

21

22

CHICAGO BEARS

Heroes Then...

The Bears are one of the NFL's oldest teams. They have had many of football's greatest heroes, too. Running back Red Grange starred in the 1920s. He was so fast and hard to catch, he was called the "Galloping Ghost." Running back Bronko Nagurski was so tough that he became a pro wrestler after his time with Chicago. **Quarterback** Sid Luckman led the Bears to four NFL championships. In the 1960s, **linebacker** Dick Butkus hammered other teams' runners, while running back Gale Sayers set scoring records. Running back Walter Payton helped the Bears win Super Bowl XX.

1920s
RED GRANGE
Running back

Walter Payton was known as "Sweetness" for his nice manners. On the field, he was toughness—a fast and powerful runner.

23

FAVORITE FOOTBALL TEAMS

Heroes Now . . .

Today's Bears have stars on both **offense** and defense. Running back Matt Forté's last name means "strength." He shows it when he runs over would-be tacklers! Devin Hester returns kicks for Chicago. He tied an all-time record with 12 kick-return **touchdowns** in his first two seasons. Fierce linebacker Brian Urlacher has been to six **Pro Bowls**. He was also the 2005 NFL defensive player of the year.

MATT FORTÉ
Running back

DEVIN HESTER
Receiver/Kick Returner

BRIAN URLACHER
Linebacker

25

FAVORITE FOOTBALL TEAMS

Gearing Up

Chicago Bears players wear lots of gear to help keep them safe. They wear pads from head to toe. Check out this picture of Brian Urlacher and learn what NFL players wear.

The Football

NFL footballs are made of four pieces of leather. White laces help the quarterback grip and throw the ball. Inside the football is a rubber bag that holds air.

Football Fact

NFL footballs don't have white lines around them. Only college teams use footballs with those lines.

- helmet
- facemask
- shoulder pad
- chest pad
- thigh pad
- knee pad
- cleats

27

FAVORITE FOOTBALL TEAMS

Sports Stats

Note: All numbers are through the 2008 season.

TOUCHDOWN MAKERS
These players have scored the most touchdowns for the Bears.

PLAYER	TOUCHDOWNS
Walter Payton	125
Neal Anderson	71

PASSING FANCY
Top Bears quarterbacks

PLAYER	PASSING YARDS
Sid Luckman	14,686
Jim Harbaugh	11,567

RUN FOR GLORY
Top Bears running backs

PLAYER	RUSHING YARDS
Walter Payton	16,726
Neal Anderson	6,166

CHICAGO BEARS

CATCH A STAR
Top Bears receivers

PLAYER	CATCHES
Walter Payton	492
Johnny Morris	356

TOP DEFENDERS
Bears defensive records

Most interceptions: Gary Fencik, 38
Most **sacks**: Richard Dent, 124.5

COACH
Most Coaching Wins

George Halas, 324

FAVORITE FOOTBALL TEAMS

Glossary

artificial fake, not real

defense players who are trying to keep the other team from scoring

end zone a 10-yard-deep area at each end of the field

field goal a three-point score made by kicking the ball between the upper goalposts

hash marks short white lines that mark off each yard on the football field

interception a catch made by a defensive player

linebacker a defensive player who begins each play standing behind the main defensive line

offense players who have the ball and are trying to score

Pro Bowls the NFL's yearly all-star games, played in February in Hawaii

quarterback the key offensive player who starts each play and passes or hands off to a teammate

receiver an offensive player who catches forward passes

rivals teams that play each other often and have an ongoing competition

running back an offensive player who runs with the football and catches passes

sacks tackles of a quarterback behind the line of scrimmage

Super Bowl the NFL's yearly championship game

touchdowns six-point scores made by carrying or catching the ball in the end zone

CHICAGO BEARS

Find Out More

BOOKS

Buckley, James Jr. *The Scholastic Ultimate Book of Football*. New York: Scholastic, 2009.

Madden, John, and Bill Gutman. *Heroes of Football*. New York: Dutton, 2006.

Polzer, Tim. *Play Football! A Guide for Young Players from the National Football League*. New York: DK Publishing, 2002.

Sandler, Michael. *Brian Urlacher: Football Heroes Making a Difference*. New York: Bearport Publishing, 2009.

Stewart, Mark. *The Chicago Bears*. Chicago: Norwood House Press, 2007.

WEB SITE

Visit our Web site for lots of links about the Chicago Bears and other NFL football teams:

childsworld.com/links

Note to Parents, Teachers, and Librarians: We routinely verify our Web links to make sure they are safe, active sites—so encourage your readers to check them out!

FAVORITE FOOTBALL TEAMS

Index

American Football
   Conference (AFC), 7
Anderson, Neal, 28
artificial grass, 15

Brown, Mike, 4
Butkus, Dick, 23

Chicago Cubs, 12
coach, 8, 15, 16, 29

Decatur Staleys, 8
defense, 4, 24, 29
Dent, Richard, 29
Detroit Lions, 11
Ditka, Mike, 16

end zone, 15

fans, 4, 11, 20
Fencik, Gary, 28
field goal, 7
football, 26
football field diagram, 14
Forté, Matt, 24

gear, 8, 26
goalposts, 15
Grange, Red, 23
Green Bay Packers, 11

Halas, George, 8, 16, 19, 29
Harbaugh, Jim, 28
hash marks, 15
history, 4, 7, 8
Hester, Devin, 24

interception, 4, 29

Layne, Bobby, 8
linebacker, 23, 24
Luckman, Sid, 8, 23, 28
Lujack, Johnny, 8

Minnesota Vikings, 11
Morris, Johnny, 29

Nagurski, Bronko, 23
National Football
   Conference (NFC), 7, 11
New England Patriots, 16
New York Giants, 16

offense, 24

Payton, Walter, 23, 28, 29
Pro Bowl, 24

quarterback, 23, 28

receivers, 29
rivals, 11
running back, 19, 23, 24, 28

sacks, 29
Sayers, Gale, 19, 23
sideline, 15
Soldier Field, 12, 15
Staley, A. E., 8
Super Bowl, 7, 16, 23

touchdowns, 24, 28

Urlacher, Brian, 11, 24, 26

Washington Redskins, 16
weather, 12, 20
Wrigley Field, 12

About the Author

K. C. Kelley is a huge football fan! He has written dozens of books on football and other sports for young readers. K. C. used to work for NFL Publishing and has covered several Super Bowls.